MEET THE AUTHOR - MICHAEL MORPURGO

What is your favourite animal?
Elephant
What is your favourite boy's name?
George
What is your favourite girl's name?
Eleanor
What is your favourite food?
Prawns
What is your favourite music?
'Spem in Alium' by Thomas Tallis
What is your favourite hobby?
Writing

MEET THE ILLUSTRATOR - JOANNA CAREY

What is your favourite animal?
My cat, Alfie
What is your favourite boy's name?
I have three favourites - Joseph, Felix and Daniel
What is your favourite girl's name?
Amy
What is your favourite food?
Smoked salmon
What is your favourite music?
Bach piano music
What is your favourite hobby?
Making things out of things

Contents

Chapter 1
Dilly Watson

I wish I'd broken my leg playing football. I'd have had a white plaster that everyone could have written their names on. Or I wish I'd been ill. Then I could have gone to hospital and everyone would have sent me cards and flowers and grapes.

But I didn't break a leg and I didn't go to hospital. I got a wart.

That sort of thing always happens to me.

I'm called Dilly, Dilly Watson. I'm Billy really, but my big brother, Jim – he's five years older than me – called me Dilly when he was little. It stuck. I've been Dilly ever since.

I didn't have warts when I was born. I didn't have warts for the first nine years of my life. My class teacher, Miss Erikson, told my mother that I was "a happy, smiley sort of boy". She didn't mean me to hear that, but I did.

That's what I *used* to be. A happy, smiley sort of boy. Then things went wrong for me, badly wrong.

Last term everything was still fine. I was in the football team. I got more votes than anyone else in the school election. I told everyone they could have everything they wanted if they voted for me – a swimming pool, free sweets and no more lessons. They didn't believe me, but they still voted for me. Well, Penny Prosser and her lot didn't, but then she's never liked me. Do you know what she said once? She said that *football was stupid*.

I've never forgiven her for that, never. But last term Penny Prosser and her lot didn't matter, because everyone else thought I was great.

Miss Erikson liked *me* best too. I could tell from the way she smiled at me. But all that, as I said, was last term, a long time ago – B.W. – Before the Wart.

Chapter 2
The Wart

A wart grows very slowly. I had this little spot on my knee. It was just a tiny, round spot. It didn't itch, so I didn't bother about it at first. Then I began to see it every night in the bath. It didn't wash off and it was always there the next night too.

Even then it didn't bother me. Everyone

has spots. Even Miss Erikson has one, on her arm, just above her watch. I've seen it.

One evening I was sitting on the sofa with my big brother Jim. We were watching TV and I was picking at the spot on my knee.

"Don't do that, Dilly," Mum said to me.

"Do what?"

"Pick at your wart. You'll get them all over your hands if you do."

"What do you mean?"

"Warts, Dilly," she said.

"Warts! I haven't got warts!"

"Only one for now, Dilly," she said. "But if you go on picking at it, it'll get bigger. And you'll get more of them."

"They're like mushrooms, Silly Dilly," said Jim. "You have to pick them in the morning."

Jim was a real pain. Mum and Dad thought so too. Which was lucky for me.

"Yuck, Jim," said Mum. And she sent him off to put some shoes on.

Jim never wore shoes in the house and Mum hated that. He played his music too loud in his room and Dad hated *that*. But I was the good guy in the family and I liked it that way.

"Don't let Jim get at you, Dilly," Mum said when he'd left the room.

"It's not a wart, is it?" I asked her.

Mum sat down beside me on the sofa and had a good look. "I think it is, Dilly. You've had it for a few weeks now. But it'll be OK. It'll go away on its own, but only if you *leave it alone*."

Jim was singing very loudly as he went upstairs, so that we could all hear. "Who's got a wart, Dilly, Dilly? ... Who's got a wart ...?"

"Jim!" Mum yelled, and he shut up.

Then I bent over to take a look at my knee, as I often did. I shook my head.

"What if it doesn't go away, Mum?" I asked.

"It will, Dilly. They always do – in the end. Just forget about it."

Jim started to sing again. "Who's got a wart, Dilly, Dilly? Who's got a wart ...?"

Mum went upstairs to sort him out.

After that I tried not to pick at the wart or to think about it. But it didn't go away, it got bigger and bigger. My spot was not a spot any more. It was a wart, and it grew harder and whiter and more crusty every day. Soon someone was going to see it at school. I didn't want to let that happen.

So this is what I did. I put a plaster over it. No-one could see it now. After all, Mum could be right, the wart might just go away.

But it didn't.

Chapter 3
Dilly's Secret

It was summer, and I was in shorts.
I begged her and I begged her, but Mum
wouldn't let me wear my jeans.

"Let your legs breathe a bit," she said.

"Legs don't breathe," I said. But she still
wouldn't let me wear jeans.

Every day, as soon as I'd left the house for school, I hid behind a tree and stuck a plaster over my wart. On the way back from school, I'd stop in the same place and rip the plaster off. Before I ripped it off, I'd shut my eyes and hope that the wart had gone. But when I opened my eyes it was still there, bigger and harder and crustier than ever. But at least my trick with the plaster worked. No-one at school knew about my wart. Not yet.

But at home, things were not going well. Jim kept on and on about my wart. He never let me forget about it. He had got a new name for me.

"Well," he said one day in the kitchen. "And how's Wartman today? Hey, Wartman, you could be a film star. *Dilly the Wartman*, that's you. So ugly you'd scare an alien."

I threw the dog bowl at him. Jim ducked and the bowl flew over his head and into the sitting room. Dad rushed into the kitchen very angry, with Mum right behind him.

"Who threw that?" he said.

Jim just grinned. "It wasn't me," Jim said.

I wanted to kick him.

"Dilly!" said Mum. "What's the matter with you?"

"He called me Wartman, Mum. He keeps on at me."

"*Silly Dilly*, or *Wartman* – what does it matter what he calls you?" said Dad. "Who cares?"

But it did matter and I did care. Mum knew that. But she didn't say anything.

And Jim went on and on about my wart. He made my life *hell*.

Chapter 4
George

In the morning, Jim would say, "Out of the bathroom, Wartman."

And then at breakfast, "Pass the milk, Wartman."

He'd even call me Wartman in front of his friends when they came to the house.

Mum was cross but she didn't stop him.
I hated that wart more and more.

I was sitting on my bed one night and
Jim's music was thumping away next door.
I was looking at my wart. Was it getting
bigger? Then Jim came in.

"Love is the only thing, Wartman," he
said, clicking his fingers to the music.

"What?"

"You've got to learn to love your wart,
Wartman," he said.

I threw a slipper at him, but it missed.

What he had said sounded stupid. But I
had a good think about it in bed that night.
What he had said just might make sense.
But how could anyone love a wart?

But my wart wasn't going to go away

the next day or the next. I was going to
have to live with it. So I gave it a name.

I called my wart 'George'. Every day
when I put the plaster over him behind the

tree, I'd say softly, "G'night, George." And when I took it off just before I got home, I'd say, "Oh, hello, George. You still there?"

And he always was there. He didn't budge.

But at school, life was getting bad. I'd worn a plaster on my knee for months now. People had started to ask about it. I'd told everyone it was a cut, that I'd fallen off my bike. I told them the cut was so deep that they'd had to rush me to hospital. I'd had four stitches. It was a good story, and I was proud of it.

It was in P.E. one day when Miss Erikson asked me, "Aren't they out yet, Dilly?"

"What, Miss?"

"Those stitches in your knee."

"Oh ... them. Yes, Miss. Last week, Miss.

The doctor took them out."

"How many did you say you had?" She gave me a funny look.

"Er ... three ... no, four, Miss. That's right, four."

It wasn't easy getting my story right each time. In the end, I was going to be found out. In the end, my 'cut' would have to get better. The plaster would have to come off.

Well, the plaster did come off, but not the way I'd planned it, not the way I'd planned it at all.

Chapter 5
The Accident

It was afternoon playtime. A few of us were kicking a ball around in the playground – the field was too wet to play on. I was dribbling the ball really well. I flew past Darren, who just stood there and stared at me. I wove around Tom and Barry.

All at once Penny Prosser was standing

there, right in my way. I tried to kick the ball round her towards the goal. And do you know what she did? She stuck her foot out and tripped me up!

I fell and rolled over and over. I ended up by the goal mouth. My knees, my elbows, my nose – everything hurt. My head was spinning. I looked up. Miss Erikson was bending over me.

"You all right, Dilly?" she asked.

I clutched my knee and I moaned and groaned. That was when I saw the plaster had gone. Instead, there was a gritty graze on my knee, hidden by my hand. A crowd was soon standing round to get a good look at me.

It was awful. I'd missed the goal. My knees and my elbows and my nose hurt. *And* the plaster had gone and there was my wart for all to see. I was about to be found out.

"Let's take a look at your knee, shall we, Dilly?" said Miss Erikson. She bent down beside me. Her hand felt cool on my leg. "I hope it hasn't opened up that cut of yours." From the way she spoke, I could tell she knew about the wart.

I put my hand over my knee again and groaned in pain. My knee did hurt a lot. I'd do anything to put off the awful moment when I'd have to take my hand away and everyone would see the wart.

"Penny tripped me up, Miss," I said. "And she wasn't even in our game. She did it to spite me, Miss. I know she did."

"No, I never," Penny told Miss Erikson. "He just ran into me, that's all. Honest, Miss."

Miss Erikson did not even look at Penny.

She was trying to pull my fingers away from my knee, but I wouldn't let her. George was there under my hand, and there was blood from the cut on my fingers.

"Come on, Dilly," she said. "I've got to see it before I know how bad it is, haven't I?"

The crowd around me looked on. There was nothing more I could do. I had to let her take away my hand.

There was George, with black plaster marks on each side of him. And there, too, was a long, red gash, like a smile.

"Oooh!" said someone.

"Bad," said someone else.

And then one of the girls saw George.

"Look, Miss, Dilly's got a great, big wart
on his knee. That's why he had that plaster
over it. You can see."

It was Penny Prosser. It had to be.

"You said you fell off your bike," said someone.

"Four stitches you told us," said someone else.

"Look, Miss." It was Penny Prosser again. She held up the plaster. "Yuck! Look what I found. Yuck!"

Things were about as bad as they could get. George had never looked so big before. The others were all grinning at me now. I was sitting there sniffing, with tears in my eyes.

It was Miss Erikson who saved me. She sent them all in and took me into the staffroom and sat me down.

"It's just a graze. You'll be fine, Dilly," she said. She got some water and cotton

wool. "I'll just clean you up a bit."

She dabbed my knee gently with warm, wet cotton wool. I was sniffing.

"Do you know what, Dilly?" she said. "I had two warts just like yours, only bigger." I thought she was just being kind. "Yes, I did, Dilly," she went on. "I had them a long time ago, just after I came to this school. They've gone now."

"But how?" I asked. "Mum said George would go, but he hasn't."

"George?" she said.

I told her my wart was called George and she smiled at me. Miss Erikson has very white teeth. I stopped sniffing. She held up her hand.

"I had one on this finger, and one on my thumb, here. One day they just went – as if they'd never been there."

It was true. There was nothing on her hand. There wasn't even a mark.

"And I'll tell you something else, Dilly.

She's so nice - I don't mind her knowing about George

I didn't give them names, but I put a plaster over them."

"Just like me?"

"Yes," she said. "You're a brave boy, Dilly."

Then she strapped a big, pink plaster over my knee.

"But how did they go? How did you get rid of them?"

"Ah, well, that's an odd story," she said. "When I tell you, you're going to think I made it all up. I'll tell you later, but let me think ... I've got an idea, Dilly. School will be over soon. I'm going to phone your mum and say that I'll bring you home myself. As soon as school's over, go and sit in my car and wait for me. We're going on a little trip."

"Where to?" I asked.

"You'll see, Dilly. You'll see."

It was hard going back into the classroom. Penny Prosser started to snigger, but Miss Erikson soon shut her up, with one flash of her eyes.

We always have a story in the last lesson. Today I didn't hear a word of it, because I was thinking. Where was Miss Erikson going to take me after school? How did *she* get rid of her warts?

Then the bell rang and it was the end of school.

Chapter 6
Mr Ben's Magic

I waited in Miss Erikson's car, just as she had told me to. I looked down at George. I rubbed away the black plaster marks. He did look a bit lonely, beside the big, new, pink plaster.

"He's still there, is he?" said Miss Erikson, as she got into the car beside me. "I phoned

your mum. She says it's OK for you to come with me."

"Where are we going, Miss?" I asked. "Is it far?"

"It's not that far," she said. "I'm going to take you to see someone who can help you. He's a nice man but he doesn't say very much. And he doesn't hear very well either. He's old and deaf. But he can magic warts away. He did it for me."

"How, Miss?"

"I don't know, Dilly. No-one knows. Does it matter?"

"You mean he's a sort of witch doctor?"

"Sort of," said Miss Erikson.

"Will it hurt, Miss?"

She smiled. "Of course not. I didn't feel a thing." And she patted my hand. "Don't be scared, Dilly."

But I was scared. We set off in the car. At last we drove into a sleepy village and stopped by the duck pond. There was a small cottage on the other side of it, with pots of flowers everywhere.

"That's his place," she said. "Mr Ben. Everyone just calls him Mr Ben. OK?"

"OK," I said.

Miss Erikson had to rap on the door again and again before he came. The door opened very slowly.

"It's me, Mr Ben," said Miss Erikson very loudly. The old man looked at her and shook his head. "I phoned, remember?" she went on. "You got rid of my warts."

He was older than anyone I'd ever seen.
Could anyone be as old as that?

He had thin, white hair, and glasses that
sat on the end of his nose. There were holes
in the toes of his slippers.

"Come in, my dear," he said.

He took us to a little room at the back of the house. It smelt musty. Everything in the room was brown. He sat down in an old, brown chair and looked at me.

Poor boy - he's scared of me

"Is this the boy?" asked Mr Ben.

"This is Dilly," said Miss Erikson loudly.

"Hello, Billy," he said. Miss Erikson and I looked at each other. Wrong name. No point in putting him right. Anyway, Billy was, in fact, my real name. He'd got it *right*. He was the first person to get it right in nine years.

"The wart is on his knee, Mr Ben," Miss Erikson went on.

Mr Ben leaned forward to look. He shook his head.

"Ooh, nasty one," he said. "They're devils, these warts. Now, I can cure a cold easily. But warts are hard to get rid of. I'll see what I can do. Come a little closer, Billy. I've got to get a good, long look at him."

I went very, very close. Mr Ben's face

was right next to my knee. He took a deep breath and then another and another.

He held my knee all the time. He gripped it hard with both hands. And he blew on my wart.

There wasn't a sound in the room. No-one moved.

Then George began to tickle. I wanted to pick at him, but I didn't dare move. Then the tickle turned into a tingle. I looked down at George. Had he gone yet? No, he was still there.

Mr Ben sat in his chair and wiped his eyes. "All done, Billy," he said.

"Thanks," I said.

"Don't thank me, Billy," smiled Mr Ben. "I haven't done much. You can't get rid of a wart, you know. All I do is send him off to feed on someone else. It's the best I can do."

I looked at him and shivered.

I thought about what Mr Ben had said all the way home.

Who would get my wart?

****

A week later, George simply went.
He wasn't there any more.

And a week after that Penny Prosser got
a wart on her finger. She says I gave her
the wart. But she would say that. I know the
truth.

And a week after that, my big brother Jim got a wart on his thumb.

Mum says Mr Ben's magic just isn't true. She still thinks Jim got my wart because he used my towel. But I know the truth, and so does Miss Erikson.

And Mr Ben didn't just get rid of my wart. He got rid of my awful nickname, Dilly, too. He called me *Billy*. I know it was by mistake, but I liked it. I liked it so much that I made up my mind that from then on I would always be called Billy.

I told everyone.

Only Jim calls me Dilly now.

From time to time he still calls me "Silly Dilly". But that's OK, I just call *him* "Wartman" back.